The
Tiara
Club

✦ *Winter Wonderland* ✦

VIVIAN FRENCH

The Tiara Club

Winter Wonderland

KATHERINE TEGEN BOOKS
HarperTrophy®
An Imprint of HarperCollins*Publishers*

The Tiara Club Winter Wonderland
Text copyright © 2008 by Vivian French
Illustrations copyright © 2008 by Orchard Books

Library of Congress Catalog Card Number: 2007904655
ISBN 978-0-06-145228-4

Typography by Amy Ryan

First U.S. edition, 2008

For Princess Angie,
with much love

xxx

—V. F.

The Royal Palace Academy
for the Preparation of Perfect Princesses
(Known to our students as "The Princess Academy")

OUR SCHOOL MOTTO:
*A Perfect Princess always thinks of others before herself,
and is kind, caring, and truthful.*

Silver Towers offers a complete education for
Tiara Club princesses with emphasis on
selected outings. The curriculum includes:

Fans and Curtseys

*A visit to Witch Windlespin
(Royal herbalist, healer, and maker of magic potions)*

Problem Prime Ministers

*A visit to the Museum of Royal Life
(Students will be well protected from the Poisoned Apple)*

Our principal, Queen Samantha Joy, is present
at all times, and students are in the excellent care
of the school Fairy Godmother, Fairy Angora.

OUR RESIDENT STAFF & VISITING EXPERTS INCLUDE:

LADY ALBINA MacSPLINTER *(School Secretary)*
CROWN PRINCE DANDINO *(Field Trips)*
QUEEN MOTHER MATILDA *(Etiquette, Posture, and Poise)*
FAIRY G. *(Head Fairy Godmother)*

We award tiara points to encourage our
Tiara Club princesses toward the next level.
All princesses who win enough points at Silver
Towers will attend the Silver Ball, where they
will be presented with their Silver Sashes.

Silver Sash Tiara Club princesses are invited
to return to Ruby Mansions, our exclusive
residence for Perfect Princesses, where they may
continue their education at a higher level.

PLEASE NOTE:
Princesses are expected to arrive
at the Academy with a *minimum* of:

TWENTY BALL GOWNS
*(with all necessary hoops,
petticoats, etc.)*

TWELVE DAY-DRESSES

SEVEN GOWNS
*suitable for garden parties
and other special daytime
occasions*

TWELVE TIARAS

DANCING SHOES
five pairs

VELVET SLIPPERS
three pairs

RIDING BOOTS
two pairs

*Cloaks, muffs, stoles, gloves,
and other essential
accessories, as required*

Hello there! Don't you just love winter? I do—with all that beautiful crunchy snow and sparkly frost, and skating on the frozen lake . . . it's so much fun!

I'm Princess Charlotte, by the way, and I know who you are! You're a Perfect Princess, and you're keeping me and my friends company at Silver Towers.

You do remember my friends, don't you? There's Katie (she likes animals) and Daisy (she's so sweet) and Alice (she's got the loveliest smile) and Sophia (she's very pretty), and Emily (who's the nicest person ever). And you!

Chapter One

$\mathcal{L}$ike I said, winter is so magical and our winter classes at Silver Towers were really special! It had been so cold for ages, but not that yucky cold that makes you feel miserable. No, it was the bright and frosty kind, and the sky always seemed to be blue. The lake in front of the Princess Academy froze over, and we had amazing skating parties. Even the horrible twins, Princess Diamonde and Princess Gruella, learned to skate, although they did tell us over and over again how very un-princessy it was.

And then the weather changed.

The first bell of the morning rang, and we opened our eyes expecting the Silver Rose Room to be bright and sunny as usual—but it wasn't. It was gray and gloomy.

Princess Daisy hopped out of bed and walked over to the window.

"It's really cloudy," she reported, "and it's pouring rain!"

Princess Katie snuggled deeper under her covers.

"The ice dancing competition was going to be this afternoon," Emily reminded us. "What'll happen now?"

We looked at each other blankly.

"Maybe the rain will stop," Princess Sophia said.

"No chance," Daisy said from the window. "It looks as if it's going to rain forever."

"That stinks." I threw my pillow at Katie, who didn't move. "We'll probably have some boring lesson instead."

Sophia stretched. "If we don't get up soon, we'll get into trouble for being late for breakfast."

Princess Alice was already heading for the bathroom. "Come on, you guys," she said. "Last one

down to breakfast has to sit with snooty old Diamonde and Gruella!"

Of course that got us moving— even Katie. We arrived at the dining hall at exactly the same time. Almost all the other princesses were already there, but

luckily we found a table where we could sit together.

Diamonde floated in a few seconds later, followed by Gruella. As they passed our table, Diamonde stuck her nose in the air.

"You must be *so* disappointed," she sneered. "No more showing off on the ice! What a shame."

"Bet they thought they'd win the competition," Gruella suggested.

Sometimes I say things before I've really thought about whether I should say them or not. Do you ever do that? Words just seem to pop out of my mouth before I can stop them.

"We can beat you at *any* competition," I said.

And at that moment, our principal, Queen Samantha Joy, came sailing into the dining hall, with our school Fairy Godmother, Fairy Angora, behind her—and the head Fairy Godmother, Fairy G., as well.

"Wow!" Sophia whispered. "Something really important must be about to happen!"

Chapter Two

Queen Samantha Joy smiled at us. "Now, my dear princesses, I'm sure you're all disappointed that there can be no ice dancing competition this afternoon. I can, however, announce another competition instead, a very special one! As you know, we are holding a Winter Festival Assembly at the end of the term, and we would like *you* to provide the entertainment."

We looked at each other in amazement.

"Think of it as a talent show," Queen Samantha Joy said. "You may work in pairs, or in a group, and on the day of the assembly, you will present a dance, or a song, or even a little play—it's up to you. And not only will it be the entertainment for your parents and friends, but it will also be a competition, and the first prize is a visit to Winter Wonderland!"

We were speechless. *Everyone* knows about Winter Wonderland— it's fantastic! There's the best ice skating rink in the whole wide world, and snow slopes with little sleds, and sleigh rides with real reindeer. And that's only some of it!

There are little wooden stalls where you can get hot chocolate with whipped cream on top, and others with crunchy spicy gingerbread, and others selling all kinds of toys and pretty things.

Then there's a Christmas Fair with a Ferris wheel covered in twinkling lights, and a carousel with the most beautiful golden horses, and games, and cotton candy stalls. And the best thing about it is that when you get there you're given a bag of silver tokens, and you pay for all the rides and presents and everything else you want with those. It's so amazing!

Of course we all began talking at once. Our teacher let us chat, but after five minutes or so, Fairy G. banged on a table with a spoon.

"Silence!" she boomed. (Fairy G. has the loudest voice ever!) "Now, here are the rules. Are you listening?"

It was so quiet you could have heard a pin drop.

"Rule number one: Each group will perform for no less than five minutes, and no more than ten.

"Rule number two: Your performance must be all your own work. If you want to recite a poem, then you must write the poem. If you want to sing a song, you must write the words and the music. If it's a play—you are the playwrights.

"Rule number three: You will also design any costumes or scenery you may need—but of course, Fairy Angora and I will be here to help in any way we can." Fairy G. stopped, and her beaming smile reached every corner of the dining hall. "And if you should need a tiny sprinkle or two of magic, I'm sure that can be arranged! Any questions?"

Diamonde had her hand up before anyone else. "Excuse me,"

she began, "but might I point out that a Perfect Princess is not expected to be an entertainer? At home, Mommy has a master of ceremonies for what she calls High Jinks and Nonsense. She says *her*

role is to be a gracious presence."

Honestly—sometimes Diamonde is so rude! We held our breath and waited for Fairy G. to explode, or for Queen Samantha Joy to be furious.

It was almost disappointing. Queen Samantha Joy just raised her eyebrows.

"So do I understand that you don't wish to take part in the competition, Princess Diamonde?" she said.

Diamonde blushed. You could tell she hadn't expected that kind of answer at all.

"Um . . ." she began. I could see

her thinking about that wonderful prize! "Um . . . well, I suppose I might . . . that is . . . I guess it would be all right for Gruella and me to take part just this once."

"Excellent," Queen Samantha Joy said briskly. "It would have been very disappointing to find that one of my princesses did not feel able to share in a festive celebration."

Fairy G. held up her wand. "Fairy Angora and I will be in the lower hall all afternoon," she said, "so if any of you need help, please come and find us there."

Fairy Angora nodded. "That's right, my little darlings. And I'll have some beautiful fabrics for your costumes!"

As our principal and the two Fairy Godmothers left the dining hall, Diamonde and Gruella came stomping over to our table. Diamonde hissed right in my face, "Remember what you said about beating us in any competition,

Princess Bragging Charlotte? Well, watch us win *this* competition and leave you in the dust!"

"So there!" Gruella said, and the two of them flounced away.

Chapter Three

"Gosh!" Sophia said, and she looked really shocked. "That's a terrible thing to say!"

Alice folded her arms. "There's only one way to deal with Diamonde and Gruella," she said. "We've got to win this competition fair and square!"

"That's right." Katie's lovely blue eyes were sparkling.

Daisy nodded in agreement, but Emily was looking thoughtful.

"Do we actually need to win?" she asked. "Wouldn't it be okay if we just do better than Diamonde and Gruella?"

"I think we go for winning," Katie said firmly. "What do you think, Charlotte?"

I remembered the way Diamonde had glared at me. "Yes," I said. "Absolutely. And if we do win, we'd get to go to Winter Wonderland too—wouldn't that be

just amazing? All of us—together?"

"It would be so fantastic." Sophia sighed.

"Do you know what? I think *that's* why we should try to win," Emily said in her quiet little voice. She blushed as we all looked at her. "Sorry. I just thought Perfect Princesses shouldn't worry about trying to teach people like

Diamonde a lesson. She's not worth worrying about."

There was a moment of silence, then Sophia gave Emily a huge hug. "You're completely and totally

right," she said, "and it only goes to prove you're the most Perfect Princess ever!"

All morning long, I kept thinking about what Emily had said, and I couldn't help feeling just a little bit awful. I was the one who had told Diamonde that we could beat her in any competition—so in a way I'd started it all, and that made me think I was not a Perfect Princess. I decided I was going to try really hard to think of others before myself.

By the time we met for lunch, we were bursting with ideas—and so was everybody else. Princess Freya actually twirled all the way down the hall, and Princess Jemima, Princess Sunita, and Princess Lisa were so deep in a discussion about their play they let their soup get cold. Princess Nancy kept singing "Tra la lala!" and Princess Eglantine

was scribbling furiously on a piece of paper.

"So," Katie said as we sat down together. "What are we going to do?"

"What about some kind of dance?" Daisy suggested. "Sophia's a wonderful dancer!"

"Or a poem?" Sophia looked at me. "You're good at rhymes, Charlotte."

"If Charlotte writes a poem, Daisy could make up a tune for it and turn it into a song," Emily said.

"And then we could dance while we sing it!" Alice's cheeks were flushed with excitement.

I gulped. "I'm not sure . . ."

"That would be perfect!" Katie clapped her hands. "You write the poem, Charlotte, and Daisy can write the music, and then Sophia can work out a dance routine! And Alice can design the costumes, and

Emily and I will help her—and we'll make some kind of back-ground as well!"

"Yes!" Alice's eyes were like stars, and everyone else was looking so

enthusiastic I didn't want to say anything. And it did sound fun . . . *if* I could write some kind of poem. . . .

"Why don't we *all* write the poem?" I said hopefully. "It's bound to be quicker that way."

"Let's start now!" Alice jumped up. "Let's go and work in the Recreation Room."

And off we went to create the best poem ever.

It wasn't that easy. We chewed the ends of our pencils for hours, but no ideas came. It didn't help that Diamonde and Gruella had followed us and were sitting on the other sofa whispering to each other.

"What about something about princesses?" I said at last.

"But what rhymes with princesses?" Daisy asked.

Alice sat up straight. "Dresses, of course!"

I began to scribble in my note-book.

We are da di da princesses
See us in our something *dresses.*

"That sounds okay," Emily said encouragingly.

Sophia looked over my shoulder. "What about, 'Silver Towers princesses'?"

"See us in our party dresses?" Daisy suggested.

"I know!" Katie grabbed the pencil out of my hand. "What about *winter* dresses? And we can put in something about snow,

and skating, and holly—"

I snatched the pencil back. "So it's a poem all about winter, and Christmas, and it could end up wishing the audience a very merry Christmas and a happy New Year!"

We all relaxed, feeling very proud of ourselves. I don't think any of us noticed how very quiet Diamonde and Gruella had suddenly become.

Chapter Four

After that, it was nonstop work, but in the best way. I wrote out our poem, and Daisy made up the tune—it was so catchy it really did make you want to dance! Sophia spent forever working out our moves, and Alice covered huge sheets of paper with designs for the most wonderful costumes.

Sophia, Emily, and Katie were to have beautiful white satin dresses with sparkly snowflakes scattered all over the skirts, and piles of fluffy petticoats. Alice, Daisy, and I would be dressed in plush dark green velvet with holly-berry red silk sashes, and our petticoats would be layers and layers of bright red silk.

"And all the dresses will have hoops under the petticoats as well," Alice told us, "so when we twirl, they'll look completely spectacular! Oh, and I want to stitch little sparkly crystals onto the green velvet, like dewdrops . . ." A dreamy look came over her face and she began to make more notes on her drawings.

"Ooooh! Look, Gruella! The horrible Silver Rose Roomers are going to have spotted dresses."

It was Diamonde, and she was staring at Alice's lovely drawings. I could see Alice wanted to hide them so Diamonde couldn't look, but she was too polite.

Gruella pushed Daisy out of the way. "What *are* those things?" she asked.

"Snowflakes," Alice said. "And now, if you'll excuse me, I'm going to choose my fabrics."

"We'd hate to get in your way," Diamonde sneered. "Of course, we've got *our* dresses planned already."

I wasn't quite sure if she was telling the truth, because a moment later, as we were walking down to the lower hall, I saw Gruella pull a notebook out of her pocket and start drawing excitedly. For a moment I wondered if she was copying Alice's ideas, but I pushed the idea out of my head. Not even the twins would be as horrible as that!

We woke up on the day of the Winter Festival feeling very excited!

We nearly bounced out of our beds. Sophia made us have one last rehearsal in our room before we went down to breakfast.

We are Silver Towers Princesses
(twirl, kick, twirl),
See us in our winter dresses
(kick, clap, kick).

We are here to wish you well
(slow curtsey).
We've got a winter tale to tell
(hold out our arms to the
audience). . . .

It went like clockwork from
beginning to end, and we finished
with:

So our wish is very clear,
a very merry Christmas,
and a happy New Year!

And as we sank into our final
curtsies, we couldn't help feeling just
a teeny bit pleased with ourselves.

Our costumes were hanging up by our beds, and they were the most wonderful dresses ever. Fairy G. and Fairy Angora had both helped. The snowflakes sparkled and the dewdrops twinkled beautifully.

Katie and Emily had made a row of little Christmas trees for the background. We *had* to win!

The Winter Festival was going to be held in the Grand Ballroom. As we hurried down the hallway in our

costumes, we could hear the hum and rustle of the audience. I knew my parents were somewhere in there, together with all the other kings and queens and princes and princesses, and I suddenly felt nervous.

When we got to the hall, Fairy G. was standing there holding a big clipboard.

"First on will be the Silver Tulip Room," she boomed. "Then Lavender, then Poppy—except for

Diamonde and Gruella; they'll go last—and so the Silver Rose Room will go after Poppy." She looked around. "Are Diamonde and Gruella here?"

"Yes, Fairy G.," Diamonde and Gruella called. They were at the back of the room, wearing huge black capes.

"What are they going to do?"

Katie whispered in my ear.

I shook my head. I hadn't seen either of them much for a couple of days. I knew they'd had their dresses specially made, because a huge package had arrived the day before, and the twins had rushed off to their room with it. Nobody had been allowed to see. Sophia had said she thought that was cheating, but apparently it was okay because they'd designed the costumes themselves.

"All right now! The rest of you tip-toe into the back of the ballroom," Fairy G. instructed us. "You can watch until it's your turn. Now, who's first? Oh, yes—the Silver Tulip Room. That's you, Jemima, isn't it? Make sure you and Lisa and Sunita and the others are ready. Good luck to you all!" We nodded and hurried away to watch the others.

The Silver Tulip Room's play was fun, although Lisa kept tripping over her long skirts. In fact, we would have enjoyed all the different performances if we hadn't been so nervous. We could see Queen Samantha Joy making notes and whispering to a very important-looking king sitting beside her, so we guessed they must be the judges.

At last there was only one group to go before us.

"Here we go!" Alice whispered in my ear.

I could hardly speak, I was so anxious. The lights dimmed, and music started to play. The crimson red curtains swept apart, and there were Diamonde and Gruella.

And one of them was dressed all in white satin with snowflakes on

her hooped skirts, and the other was in green velvet with a holly-berry red silk sash!

They curtsied to the audience, who were clapping loudly, and Gruella began to chant:

We are Silver Towers Princesses.
See us in our winter dresses!

Diamonde went on:

We are here with a very clever
story to tell.
And we hope you will think
we are doing it very well!

It was awful! It was almost exactly what we'd planned, except we had a better tune and they

didn't dance—they just marched up and down. But it was everything we'd thought of. I felt totally sick. How could we go on now? Everyone

would laugh! There was a huge lump at the back of my throat and I was close to bursting into tears.

And then Diamonde stopped.

Honestly. After just two lines.

She stopped suddenly and looked like a rabbit that had seen the scariest wolf in the whole wide world. She had obviously forgotten her words. The audience began to shift in their seats, and Diamonde looked more and more desperate. I knew she must be wanting the floor to swallow her up.

And that's when I knew what I had to do. I stood up in the back of the Grand Ballroom, and I sang in my loudest voice:

We are Silver Towers Princesses.
See us in our winter dresses!

And I twirled and kicked my legs
as I danced up the middle of
the central aisle in the Grand

Ballroom. I knew my friends were following because I could hear them singing with me.

We are here to wish you well—

we sang, and as we reached the
front of the stage, we curtsied to
Diamonde and Gruella.

We've got a winter tale to tell . . .

We climbed up the steps, and as we held out our hands to the audience, the twins unfroze and copied us.

On we sang, and we danced like we'd never danced before, and we spun Diamonde and Gruella around so it really looked as if they

knew what they were doing. At the end, we sang,

So our wish is very clear,
a very merry Christmas,
and a happy New Year!

and sank into the deepest curtsies, and Diamonde and Gruella curtsied with us.

The applause was amazing! Everybody there clapped and cheered, and we curtsied and curtsied until at last the curtain fell. And as it fell, the weirdest thing happened.

Gruella turned bright red and stamped her foot and shouted at Diamonde.

"I told you we shouldn't copy what they did! I knew you'd forget the words!"

For a moment, none of us knew what to do. I could see Fairy G. and Fairy Angora, and Fairy Angora was looking shocked. Fairy G. wasn't, though. She didn't look surprised at all.

And then Diamonde squealed and rushed off the stage, and Gruella ran after her.

When it came to the grand finale, and we were asked to come onto the stage for the results of the competition, neither of the twins was there.

Chapter Six

𝒯here was a burst of trumpets, and Queen Samantha Joy stood up. "My dear princesses," she began. She sounded very pleased and proud. "You have outdone your-selves, and I wish it were possible for every single one of you to go to

Winter Wonderland. Unfortunately, the prize is for one group only . . . and it gives me great pleasure to announce the winner."

She paused, and we all held our breath—although I knew we weren't going to win. How could we? Our presentation had gotten all mixed up with Diamonde and Gruella's.

"We have chosen the winners for a very special reason," our principal went on. "Here at Silver Towers, we believe the most important lesson we can teach is that Perfect Princesses should always think of others before themselves. Tonight there has been a wonderful demonstration of just such thought. We award the first prize to . . . the Silver Rose Room!"

For a moment, we stood completely still. Then we screamed. I know—Perfect Princesses do not scream, but we did. We just couldn't

help it. And then we hugged each other and curtsied to Queen Samantha Joy and waved to our parents and grandparents. The audience went wild. They clapped and clapped

and clapped, and we curtsied over
and over again. It was wonderful!

That night, as we lay tucked up in
our beds in the Silver Rose Room,

Alice asked, "Does anyone know what happened to Diamonde and Gruella?"

"Freya's mom told my mom they've been sent home," Sophia said sleepily. "She said Gruella admitted to Fairy G. that she'd copied Alice's pictures, and after that Diamonde confessed that she'd cheated."

"Oh, well," Katie said. "It turned out all right in the end."

"Thanks to Charlotte," Emily said and blew me a kiss.

"The Perfect Princess," Daisy added.

And as I sank into sleep, I knew

that no dream could ever be as wonderful as my real life.

Five wonderful friends, and you—and we're all going to Winter Wonderland!

Hello! Isn't it exciting? We're going to Winter Wonderland! Hurray, hurray, and double hurray! And it's wonderful that you're coming too. It wouldn't be the same without you.

I'm Princess Alice. Did you guess? And you've met Charlotte, Katie, Daisy, Emily, and Sophia—so all we have to do now is enjoy ourselves! I mean, what could possibly go wrong when we're all on a trip together?

Chapter One

$\mathscr{A}$t first we couldn't believe it when we won the trip to Winter Wonderland. Even when we were in the coach and on our way, it didn't seem real. It was only as we swept through the sparkly gates that we suddenly realized—here we were!

It was so exciting!

Outside the gates, it was an ordinary sort of drizzly day, but inside, the sky was blue and the sun was shining. And the ground was covered in snow—snow as white as the best frosting.

We all began to talk at once and tell each other what we could see out of the windows. Fairy G. and Fairy Angora, who'd come along to chaperone, laughed.

"Isn't it beautiful?" Fairy G. beamed. "And are you looking forward to staying in an ice palace, my dears?"

We were completely silent.

"An ice palace?" Princess
Charlotte said at last, her eyes wide.
"That's right," Fairy G. said.
"Look, you can just see the towers!"

We rushed to the side of the coach, and there were these magical ice towers soaring into the clear blue sky. They were so sparkly we couldn't look at them for long— they were truly dazzling!

"Isn't it really cold inside?" Princess Emily asked.

Fairy Angora shook her head. "I don't know how they do it, but it's actually warm and cozy. The bedrooms all have furry white rugs and glowing lanterns—you'll love them, my little darlings."

A thought popped into my head: "Will we be in a dorm room—like at school?"

"Oh, I hope so," Princess Katie said. "It won't be half as much fun if we're in separate rooms."

Fairy G. and Fairy Angora looked at each other, and I knew something wasn't quite right.

Fairy G. said, "The rooms sleep five, not six, so we'll have to put one of you in a single room next door."

"Oh!" Katie sounded surprised. "But how will we choose who has the single room?"

Fairy Angora smiled her lovely

smile. "I've thought it all out," she said and she fished a bunch of folded pieces of paper out of her bag. "One of these has a little bed drawn on it—and the person who chooses that one gets the single room!" She piled the papers onto the seat of the coach, and we each

took one—and guess what?

I had the picture of the little bed. "It's me," I said. I suddenly felt as if I was going to cry.

Is that babyish? It probably is, and not at all what a Perfect Princess should do. But I know what fun we have when we're all together, and I didn't want to be left out.

"You can be in our room right until we have to go to sleep," Charlotte promised.

"We'll miss you terribly!" Princess Daisy said, and Katie and Emily nodded in agreement.

"Of course we will, but you'll be

right next door, and we can leave our doors open." Princess Sophia gave my arm a comforting little squeeze.

I began to feel better. And just at that moment, we passed a sleigh full of happy-looking people. The sleigh was pulled by six reindeer, with red velvet harnesses covered in tinkling bells! It looked like so

much fun, I forgot about being on my own.

"What shall we do first?" Fairy G. asked. "Would you like to take a sleigh ride so we can see where everything is?"

"Oh, yes, please!" we all said together, and the coach stopped. We were in front of the ice palace, and it looked amazing. We tumbled out and hurried through the glittering front door. A tall footman dressed in red and green bowed to us as we entered.

"You must be the Silver Towers Princesses," he said. "Welcome to the Ice Palace at Winter Wonderland! Please follow me to your rooms."

Chapter Two

*F*airy Angora was right. The palace was wonderfully warm and beautiful. There were thick rugs scattered over the polished wooden floors, and ruby lanterns glowed from every shelf. You could only tell the palace was made of ice

when you looked up to the ceiling
and saw these amazing frills and
rosettes and curlicues all carved out
of ice!

When we got upstairs, it was just
as nice. The footman showed Fairy

G. and Fairy Angora to their room, and they both had the most elegant-looking beds piled with velvet cushions.

"Fairy Angora and I will get ready," Fairy G. announced, "and

then we'll be off."

My friends' room was the next door along the hall—there were many doors—and that was gorgeous too. All the beds were four-

posters, with the prettiest pink silk and satin patchwork covers, and in the corner was a huge comfy sofa piled high with cushions. The windows looked out over the snowy

slopes. There were lots of sleds whizzing downhill—and then we saw little snow-white ponies waiting patiently at the bottom to tow the sleds back up again. We could hardly believe our eyes. It was perfect!

"Can we please go sledding?" I begged. "It looks like so much fun!"

"We're going to do everything!" Katie said. "That's why we're here!"

The footman coughed politely. "Excuse me, Your Highness," he said, "but would you like to see your room?"

"Oh!" I said. I'd forgotten I wasn't going to be in the big room. "Yes. Thank you very much."

He picked up my suitcase, and I followed him. But my room wasn't next door at all. It was at the other end of the hallway.

It was a very nice room. If I'd been staying in the Ice Palace with my grandparents I'd have loved it, but it did feel different from the girls' room. It had a nice bed with a draped sky-blue canopy, but I knew that when I woke up in the morning I'd feel really lonely. The footman bowed, and left me, and I

slowly began to put my things away, thinking about how Katie and Charlotte and the others would be chattering and laughing together.

Suddenly I remembered something. The big comfy sofa! I'd ask

Fairy G. if I could sleep there! Halfway out the door, I stopped. What if Fairy G. was changing? Or not in her room anymore? On the top of the chest of drawers was some writing paper and a pencil. Before I could change my mind, I took a sheet of paper, and wrote:

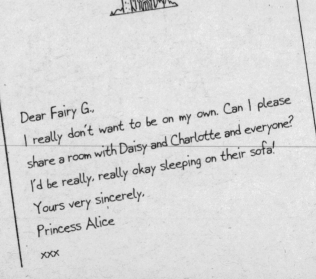

Dear Fairy G.,
I really don't want to be on my own. Can I please share a room with Daisy and Charlotte and everyone? I'd be really, really okay sleeping on their sofa!
Yours very sincerely,
Princess Alice

xxx

I folded the paper in half and ran back down the hallway. All the doors were shut, but I was sure I remembered which was Fairy G.'s room. I slipped my letter under her door. It caught on something for a second, but then it was gone. I skipped back to my room feeling much better. I was so certain Fairy G. would say yes, I didn't even put my pajamas under my pillow.

I won't tell the others yet, I decided. *I'll let it be a surprise.*

A couple of minutes later, Fairy Angora knocked on my door. "Time to go, Princess Alice," she called. I grabbed my coat and muff and hurried out.

Fairy G., Charlotte, Emily, Sophia, and Katie were already sitting in the sleigh. I gave Fairy G. a hopeful look, but she was busy arranging a fluffy blanket over her knees and didn't notice.

I squeezed in next to Charlotte and sighed happily. "Isn't this the best?"

Charlotte grinned. "It would be

if you didn't take up so much room!"

Fairy Angora looked almost as excited as we did. "Are we all here?" she asked. "Oh! Where's Princess Daisy?"

"She was in the bathroom when we came downstairs," Emily said. "She said she'd follow us."

"Should I go and look for her?" I suggested.

But just then, Daisy appeared—and she looked as if she'd been crying.

Chapter Three

Of course we asked Daisy what was wrong, but she wouldn't say. Instead she blew her nose and said she was fine.

The only empty seat was opposite me, but instead of sitting right down Daisy gave me an odd look. It was almost as if she was angry with me. Then she squeezed in next to Emily. It was so unlike her, I didn't know what to think.

"Off we go!" Fairy G. said cheerfully, and the driver shook the reins. The bells rang a little tune, and the reindeer began to trot

along the snow-covered road.

We went up and down the sledding slopes, and we couldn't help laughing at the rosy-cheeked toddlers who were playing around and making snow angels. Then we went past the ice rink, and it was so wonderful it almost made me want

to jump out of the sleigh then and there. If I'd had my skates, I would have. Then we came to the Christmas Fair, and the very first

thing we saw was the Ferris wheel. It was enormous!

"You can see all of Winter Wonderland from the top," Fairy Angora told us, and Charlotte and I smiled at each other. We couldn't wait.

"Would anyone like a cup of hot chocolate?" Fairy G. asked as we began to wind our way in between the little wooden stalls. "You could have a look around as well, if you like." She bent down to dig into her huge basket and pulled out six sparkling silver bags.

"Here are your Wonderland tokens. You can pay for anything

you want with these. No money is
needed."

I heaved another huge sigh of
happiness. It was fantastic. And I
knew just what I wanted to buy. I
wanted to find the best Christmas
presents ever for all my best friends.

But first, we had to pat the reindeer. They lowered their heads so
we could scratch them behind their
big furry ears. Their eyes were huge

and they almost seemed to be smil-
ing at us.

"Hot chocolate!" Fairy G. said
firmly and shooed us toward the

nearest stall. I stopped to wait for Daisy and Emily, but Daisy hurried past me and went to talk to Sophia. I was really surprised, and Emily looked puzzled too.

"Is Daisy okay?" I asked. Emily rubbed her nose.

"I don't know," she said. "Something's upset her, but she won't say what."

"But we always tell each other everything," I said.

Emily nodded. "I know." She hesitated, and blushed. "I think it might have something to do with you, Alice."

"Me?" I stared at Emily, and then I remembered how Daisy had looked at me when she got into the sleigh.

But what could I have done?

I felt awful. We'd all been best friends forever. I decided it must be some kind of misunderstanding, but there was only one way to find out for sure. I had to find Daisy and ask her, but when I got to the chocolate stall she wasn't there.

"She's gone to do some secret Christmas shopping," Fairy G. said when I asked her where Daisy was. She handed me a big mug of steaming hot chocolate, covered with

thick whipped cream and chocolate sprinkles. "Sophia's gone as well, but in the other direction. We're all meeting back here in an hour."

"Actually, I'd love to do some secret shopping," I said. I could see some beautiful little bags hanging outside a stall just a little way away,

and I was dying to have a good look. I also thought I could look for Daisy, and maybe we could talk, and I could find out what was wrong.

"Can I go too?" Katie's eyes were sparkling. "I want to buy some very secret things!"

"And me!" Charlotte said, and Emily nodded.

"The sleigh will be back here about three o'clock," Fairy G. said. "Don't be late!"

"We won't," we promised. I wandered away, sipping my chocolate as I went.

Chapter Four

*I*t was so hard to choose. All the little bags were perfect, but then I saw some pretty scarves, and then there were some really nice necklaces and bracelets. It took me forever to make up my mind, but in the end I bought a silver charm bracelet for each of my friends. I found an especially nice one for Daisy—it had tiny silver-and-white enamel daisies, and it was very sweet. I knew she'd love it.

I got back to the chocolate stall just in time. Fairy G. was already beginning to stomp around and

look at her watch in a very obvious way.

"Sorry!" I panted as I stuffed my packages into the sleigh.

"Harrumph!" Fairy G. said. "Well, you're not the very last. Has anyone seen Princess Daisy?"

None of us had.

Fairy G. made a face. "We'll give her a few more minutes," she said. "After all, we are on vacation."

But Daisy didn't come back.

After twenty minutes we were getting really worried. It wasn't like Daisy; she's usually on time for everything.

"Do you think the poor little darling could have gotten lost?" Fairy Angora asked.

Sophia shook her head. "None of us did," she pointed out. "It's really easy to find your way around—there are signs everywhere."

"She was looking as if she'd been

crying when she came out of the
Ice Palace," Katie said thoughtfully.
"As if something had upset her."

"But what could it be?" Fairy G.
asked. "She was bursting with
excitement in the coach on the way
here."

I swallowed hard. "Emily thinks it might be something I've done."

"You?" Everyone stared at me in surprise, and then turned to Emily.

Emily blushed. "It was just that Daisy was reading a piece of paper in our room," she said, "and I thought it looked like Alice's writing. Daisy stuffed it in her pocket when she saw me looking and rushed into the bathroom."

Have you ever been accused of something, and you know you haven't done anything wrong, but you still feel guilty? It was weird. I felt awful. All my friends were looking at me, and so were Fairy G.

and Fairy Angora. I could feel myself beginning to blush.

"The only thing I've written was my note to Fairy G.," I said. "Honestly!"

Fairy G. raised her eyebrows. "A note to me, Princess Alice?"

I nodded. "Yes, asking if I could sleep on the sofa in the room with all my friends."

"But I never got a note," Fairy G. said. "Are you sure you haven't made a mistake?"

Chapter Five

I felt hot and cold all at the same time, and my mind began to go in little circles. For a second I wondered if I could have written a mean note to Daisy without knowing I'd done it, but I knew I hadn't.

I took a deep breath. "Fairy G.,"

I said, "I really did write you a note. I don't know what Daisy was reading, but it absolutely wasn't anything from me. I think we need to find her, and then we can ask her what's going on."

Fairy G. gave me one of her piercing stares, where you feel as if she's looking right into the back of your head. Then she nodded.

"Very well said, Princess Alice. You're right. I'll stay here, and Fairy Angora will take the sleigh back to the Ice Palace in case Daisy's gone there. The five of you have a good look around, but please come back to check with me every fifteen minutes."

It was so sad; none of us felt happy anymore—we were so worried about poor Daisy. Charlotte took my arm as we hurried away.

"Don't worry," she said. "We all know you'd never do anything to upset Daisy."

"That's right." Katie and Sophia and Emily were right behind me. "In half an hour we'll be sitting on top of the Ferris wheel with Daisy and wondering what the fuss was all about!"

It was very kind of them, but it almost made me feel worse. Then I realized what Katie had said.

"The Ferris wheel!" I shouted. "Katie, you're a genius! Fairy Angora said you can see all of Winter Wonderland from the top. We'll be able to see where Daisy is!"

We rushed toward the wheel, and it felt like hours before it eventually stopped and we could get on.

We settled ourselves in our sky boat, and the wheel began to turn again.

"Katie and Charlotte, you look that way," I instructed. "Emily and Sophia, if you look at the other side, I'll look straight ahead."

Up we went, up and up—it was just like flying! We were so high, my stomach began to fill with butterflies, and I was glad to see Sophia was gripping the rail almost as tightly as I was.

And then I saw Daisy. She was sitting all by herself behind the cotton candy stall, and she looked very lonely.

"There she is!" I yelled.

Of course we had to wait for the wheel to stop before we could get

off, and that seemed to take hours as well. We scrambled out and dashed for the cotton candy stall, and were just in time to see Daisy get up and slowly walk away.

"Daisy!" we shouted, "Daisy! Come back!"

Daisy turned around, and we could see she'd been crying again. Her little nose was bright red and

she was clutching a soggy tissue in one hand. In the other was a torn piece of scribbled-on paper—and I saw my own handwriting!

Chapter Six

"Daisy!" I puffed as I ran to her. "Daisy—what's that piece of paper?"

For a moment I thought she was going to run away, but she didn't. She sniffed and handed me the paper.

"I never guessed you didn't like me," she said and began to sob.

I stared at the paper, and Charlotte and Katie looked over my shoulder while Sophia and

Emily put their arms around Daisy and gave her a clean tissue.

"Oh, Daisy!" I said—and I didn't know if I should laugh or cry. "This is my note to Fairy G.—I must have put it under the wrong door! And it's only half of it! I was asking if I could sleep on the sofa in

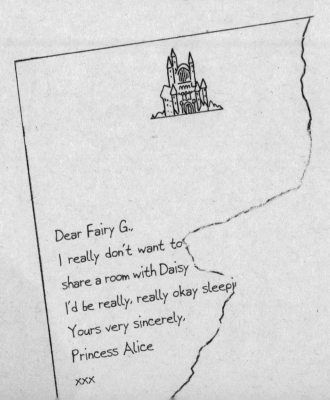

Dear Fairy G.,
I really don't want to
share a room with Daisy
I'd be really, really okay sleep'
Yours very sincerely,
Princess Alice
xxx

your room because I didn't want to be on my own and be left out."

Daisy's eyes grew wider and wider—and then she gave me the biggest hug. We all began to laugh, and as we hurried back to Fairy G.,

we linked arms and continued laughing. All of a sudden we were back to being the Tiara Club on vacation, and I'm absolutely certain the others felt as happy as I did.

Fairy G. laughed too when we

told her what had happened, and seconds after we'd arrived, Fairy Angora came swooshing over the snow in the sleigh, waving a crumpled piece of paper.

"I found this caught under the

girls' door," she said, "and I was sure it was a clue!"

It was the other half of my note. When Daisy read the two pieces together, she just couldn't stop hugging me.

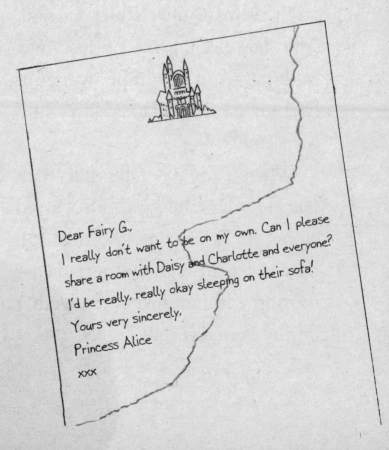

Dear Fairy G.,
I really don't want to be on my own. Can I please share a room with Daisy and Charlotte and everyone? I'd be really, really okay sleeping on their sofa!
Yours very sincerely,
Princess Alice

xxx

"I'm so sorry, Alice," she kept saying.

And I kept saying I was sorry too, until Fairy G. boomed, "Enough!"

We were very quiet.

"It seems to me," Fairy G. said, "this has been a lot of fuss over nothing! And it's time we went back to the Ice Palace. Hurry into the sleigh!"

When Fairy G. talks like that, you do what she says, but we did enjoy the ride home. We made all kinds of plans for the next day— starting with another ride together on the Ferris wheel!

And when we got back to the Ice Palace, guess what Fairy G. did?

Yes! You're right.

She waved her wand, and the big squishy sofa in the dormitory suddenly turned into a cute little bed.

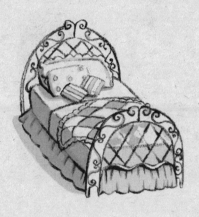

"Sssh!" she said and put her finger to her lips. "Don't tell anyone. And remind me to change it back when we leave."

We promised, and then we hurried to change into our very best evening gowns for the Ice Palace Welcome Ball.

Did we dance until midnight?
Of course we did!
And as the clock struck twelve,
we gave each other our presents,

and Daisy absolutely loved her bracelet.

"Tiara Club forever!" Katie cheered.

"Yes," I agreed, "and best friends forever as well!"

And that means you too . . . and I do hope we see you again soon.

You are cordially invited
to the Royal Princess Academy.

Introducing the new class of princesses
at Ruby Mansions

Katherine Tegen Books
An Imprint of HarperCollinsPublishers

HarperTrophy®
An Imprint of HarperCollinsPublishers